Spot Goes to the Circus

Eric Hill

PUFFIN BOOKS

Here we

are at the circus.
Fetch your ball,
Spot.

It's okay,
Mom.
I've got it!

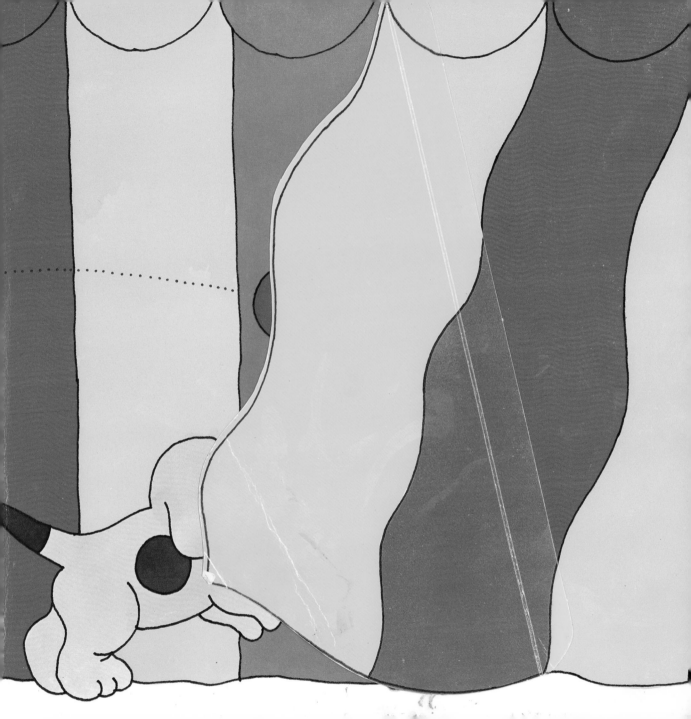

There it goes! I wonder who lives in here.

Please,
do you have
my ball?

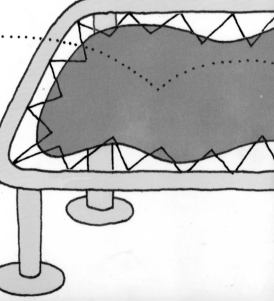

I hope you didn't swallow my ball.

There it is!

Have you seen my ball?

At last! Spot has found his ball.

That's a neat trick!

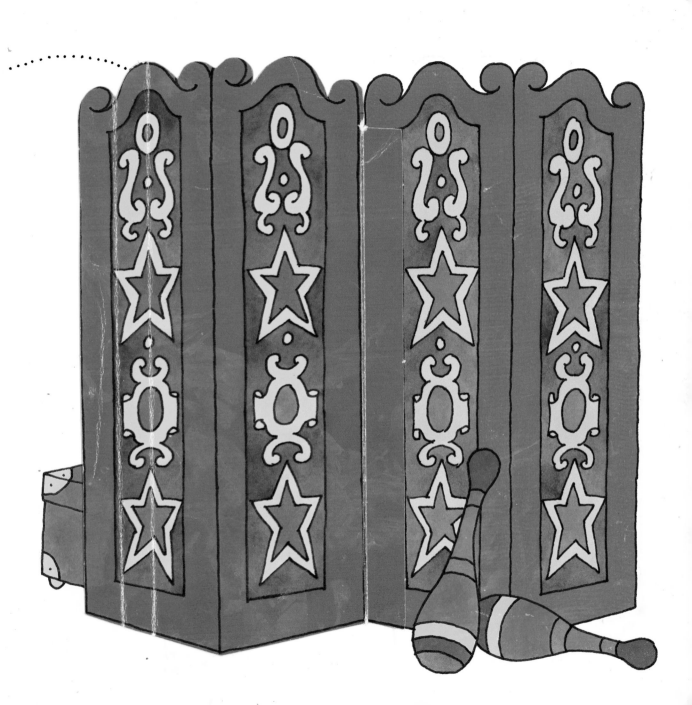

Spot

Who taught you how to do that?

My friend
the seal.
It's easy!

PUFFIN BOOKS

Published by the Penguin Group: London, New York,
Australia, Canada, India, New Zealand and South Africa
Penguin Books Ltd, Registered Offices:
80 Strand, London WC2R 0RL, England

www.penguin.com

First published by William Heinemann Ltd, 1986
Published in Puffin Books 1989
This colorized edition published in the United States of America by Puffin Books,
a division of Penguin Books for Young Readers, 2006

5 7 9 10 8 6 4

Printed and bound in Malaysia

ISBN 13: 978–0–14240–567–3